Scrambled Eggs

5 DINOSAUR DETECTIVE
Scrambled Eggs

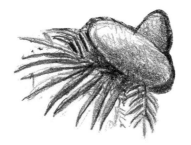

B. B. Calhoun

illustrated by Daniel Mark Duffy

Scientific
BOOKS FOR YOUNG READERS
American

W. H. FREEMAN AND COMPANY ◆ NEW YORK

Book design by Debora Smith

Scientific American Books for Young Readers is an imprint of
W. H. Freeman and Company, 41 Madison Avenue
New York, New York 10010

This book was reviewed for scientific accuracy by Don Lessem, founder of The Dinosaur Society.

Library of Congress Cataloging-in-Publication Data

Calhoun, B. B., 1961–

Scrambled eggs / B. B. Calhoun.

—(Dinosaur detective; #5)

Summary: Fenton Rumplemayer discovers a fossilized dinosaur nest at his father's archaeological dig outside Morgan, Wyoming, but has to solve the mystery of why the dinosaur remains there are much too large for the eggs that were laid.

ISBN 0-7167-6584-5 (hard)—ISBN 0-7167-6585-3 (pbk.)

[1. Dinosaurs—Fiction. 2. Eggs—Fiction. 3. Paleontology—Fiction. 4. Mystery and detective stories.] I. Title. II. Series: Lowenstein, Christina. Dinosaur detective; #5.

PZ7.C12744Sc 1995

[Fic]—dc20   94-34186
                                                          CIP
                                                          AC

Printed in the United States of America.

10 9 8 7 6 5 4 3 2 1

1

"Hey, come on, you guys," said Fenton Rumplemayer. "Let's go play Ping-Pong now."

"In a minute, Fen," answered his friend Maggie Carr, burying her nose deeper into the *Wild Stallion* comic book she was reading.

"Mmm," said Willy Whitefox, who was seated nearby reading another comic book. "Later."

Fenton stood up from the wooden crate he had been sitting on and stubbed the toe of his sneaker against the floor impatiently. It was Friday, and Fenton, his dog, Owen, Maggie, and Willy had been hanging around the old wooden shack where Willy kept his comic book collection all afternoon. Maggie, who loved horses, was deep in the *Wild Stallion* adventure, and Willy was busy reading some new comic series that he was really into.

If only Willy had some comic books about dinosaurs, thought Fenton. Now *those* would be fun to read. Fenton loved dinosaurs; in fact, he was pretty much an expert on them. Both of his parents were paleontologists—scientists who study fossils—and Fenton had been around dinosaur bones ever since he was just a little kid.

At first Fenton had learned about dinosaurs from books and from visiting the New York Museum of Natural History, where both of his parents had worked. But then, last summer, his mother had gotten a grant to study fossils in India for a year, and his father had been sent out to Morgan, Wyoming, to head a dinosaur dig site on nearby Sleeping Bear Mountain. Fenton had moved from New York City to Morgan with his father, and now he got to see dinosaur bones being dug out of the ground at Sleeping Bear all the time. In fact, Fenton, Willy, and Maggie often helped with the excavations, and Fenton had even managed to solve a few dinosaur mysteries for his father's paleontological dig team.

Fenton reached down to stroke Owen behind the ears. Reading comic books in the shack was okay, for a while, but he was getting kind of bored. And the thought of the brand-new Ping-Pong table down in Willy's basement was making him even more restless.

"Come on, you guys," he said again. "Let's go play."

"Okay," said Maggie, slapping shut her comic. "Finished. Willy, you ready?"

"Wow," said Willy, still reading. "This is really something. Did you know that there was a house in Briggton, Maine, with five ghosts that played the piano every night?"

"What are you talking about?" said Maggie.

"It's all right here," said Willy, pointing to his comic book. "The name of the house was Whispering Pines, and the family that lived there was finally driven out by the ghosts."

"What is that you're reading?" asked Fenton.

Willy held up the comic book. On the cover was a picture of an old-fashioned mirror with a fancy gold frame. Reflected in the mirror was a translucent white ghostlike creature with glowing green eyes. The title was *Ghostimonials: Absolutely TRUE Tales of the Supernatural, Volume 3*.

"I don't know, Willy," said Fenton. "I'd think twice before I believed a comic book, if I were you."

"But these stories are all supposed to be real," Willy said. "It's guaranteed, right on the back page of every issue."

"Let me see that," said Maggie.

Willy handed her the comic.

"This doesn't mean anything," she said, scanning the back page. "All it says here is that the stories are guaranteed to have been told to the authors by people who *claim* that these things actually happened to them."

"There!" said Willy triumphantly. "See?"

Maggie shook her head. "Willy, you don't mean to say that you actually *believe* this stuff, do you?"

"Really," said Fenton. "Everybody knows there's no such thing as ghosts and haunted houses."

"Besides," said Maggie, flipping through the comic book,

"this entire story's filled with holes. Listen to this." She began to read. "'*Every evening at exactly the same time, the woman heard the family's piano begin to play down in the drawing room. She rushed downstairs, but when she got there, the piano was always silent, and no one was ever there.*'" She looked up. "That's ridiculous. If the piano always started playing at exactly the same time every night, why didn't she just wait in the drawing room for it to start, instead of running downstairs like that?"

"Really," said Fenton. "And if she never actually saw any of these ghosts playing, how did she know that there were five of them? By the way they played? That's kind of hard to believe."

"Well, I still think it could be true," said Willy stubbornly. "I mean, they wouldn't say it unless it was."

"Believe me, there's no such thing as ghosts," said Fenton confidently. "If there were, there'd be some scientific proof."

"Right," agreed Maggie. "People have been telling ghost stories for ages, but none of it means a thing without evidence."

"It's just like out at the dig site," said Fenton. "When my dad and the others dig up fossils, that's evidence of how the dinosaurs lived and died. Paleontologists could just *guess* about that stuff, but without fossils, they would never have any evidence to help prove their theories."

"Well, okay, how about this for evidence," said Willy. "I read in another issue of *Ghostimonials* about this woman who used to bake a cherry pie every Saturday morning using fresh cherries from the tree outside her kitchen window. It was her husband's favorite dessert."

"Maybe *he* should have been doing the baking, then," said Maggie.

"Whatever," said Willy. "That's not the point. The point is that when the husband died, the woman was so upset she said she'd never bake another cherry pie again." Willy paused dramatically. "That is, until the next Saturday morning, when she looked out her kitchen window and saw that every single one of the cherries had fallen off her tree."

"So?" said Maggie.

"Don't you see?" said Willy. "It's like the husband was trying to send her a message. He wanted her to bake a pie."

"But that doesn't even make any sense," said Fenton. "Why would he want a pie if he's dead? It's not like he can eat it."

"I don't know," said Willy. "Maybe he missed the way it smelled or something. Anyway, don't you see? The evidence is the cherries. I mean, *something* had to make them all fall off the tree like that, right?"

"How about an unexpected frost that killed the fruit overnight?" suggested Maggie. "And speaking of which, how could this woman have baked a pie every single Saturday with fresh cherries in the first place? Cherry trees don't have fruit on them year round, you know."

"Good point," said Fenton.

"Okay, forget it, you guys," said Willy. "You don't have to believe it if you don't want to. But I still think it could be true."

"I'll tell you what I do believe," said Maggie with a grin. "I believe it's *your* turn to lose at Ping-Pong, Fenton."

"Oh, yeah?" said Fenton, heading toward the door of the shack. "What makes you so sure you're going to win?"

"Simple," said Maggie, following him. "Evidence. I usually win, don't I?"

Willy put the issue of *Ghostimonials* on top of a stack of comics in the corner, and the three of them stepped outside into the woods.

"She's right," he said to Fenton. "She almost always beats you."

"Well, she beats you a lot too, Willy," Fenton pointed out.

Fenton had to admit, Maggie did win a lot of the games. The three of them had a system—whoever won the last game automatically got to play the odd one out in the next game. Sometimes it seemed like Maggie got to play a lot more than anyone else.

"What's your secret, anyway, Maggie?" asked Willy. "Does your family have a Ping-Pong table hidden away somewhere on the ranch that you haven't told us about?"

"What's my secret?" Maggie repeated as they made their way through the woods toward Willy's house. "Why, you ought to know, Willy."

"What do you mean?" he asked her.

"Yeah," said Fenton. "What does Willy have to do with it?"

Maggie stopped walking, raised her eyebrows, and glanced quickly from side to side.

"Well," she said in a hushed voice, "whenever I play, a strange, eerie, unexplainable thing happens."

"Oh yeah?" said Willy, leaning closer.

"That's right," said Maggie, nodding ominously. "As soon as I pick up the paddle, my body gets taken over by the ghost of a former Ping-Pong champion!" She laughed.

Fenton laughed too, and Owen barked.

"All right, all right, you guys. Very funny," said Willy. "Maybe you're right. Maybe there's no such thing as ghosts after all. But I could be right too, you know. For all we know, those stories in *Ghostimonials* could be absolutely true."

Fenton shook his head. There was one thing he was sure of, and that was that anyone who believed in ghosts must have quite an imagination.

"Come on," he said, picking up his pace. "Enough ghost stories. Let's go play."

2

"Fenton! Fenton!" called a voice from the backyard.

"There's Willy," said Fenton, standing up from the breakfast table and walking over to the kitchen window, as Owen started barking. Fenton rapped on the glass and motioned for Willy to come inside.

"Are you finished with this, son?" asked Mr. Rumplemayer, picking up Fenton's cereal bowl from the table.

"Yeah. Thanks, Dad," said Fenton.

Willy banged through the side door and walked into the kitchen.

"Hi," he said to Fenton. "Hi, Mr. Rumplemayer."

"Hello, Willy," said Mr. Rumplemayer. "Have you had breakfast yet?"

Willy nodded. "I'm stuffed. I must have had about twelve pancakes."

At the mention of pancakes, Fenton couldn't help feeling a little jealous. Meals at Willy's house were always great. Both of his parents were good cooks, and they never seemed to eat anything frozen or out of a can, the way Fenton and his father sometimes did.

"Okay, then," said Mr. Rumplemayer. "Do you boys still want to go out to the dig site?"

"Yeah," said Willy.

"Definitely," said Fenton, slipping into his wool baseball jacket.

Fenton loved going to Sleeping Bear Mountain. Looking for fossils could be a long, painstaking process, but as far as Fenton was concerned, it was worth it. There was nothing like the feeling of digging up a bone or a tooth and knowing that it was millions and millions of years old.

"Maggie wants to go too," he added. "I told her we'd stop in front of the ranch on our way and pick her up."

"All right," said Mr. Rumplemayer. He pulled on his own jacket and headed out of the kitchen, with the boys and Owen behind him. "It's just that it looks a little like rain. And I'm afraid things aren't too exciting out there right now. You know we haven't found a single fossil since the dilophosaurus."

Recently Fenton's father and the other paleontologists at Sleeping Bear had uncovered part of a Jurassic dinosaur that had somehow mysteriously ended up in rock from the Cretaceous, a period that came millions of years later. No one had been able to understand it until Fenton, with some help from his friends, had come up with the answer.

"Don't worry. We won't be bored," said Fenton as they all made their way outside to the green pickup truck in the driveway. "Come on, Owen," he said, motioning the dog into the back of the truck.

"Anyway," said Willy to Mr. Rumplemayer, "that's why we're going, to help you look for fossils."

"Well, I suppose you might as well," said Mr. Rumplemayer. He opened the door to the pickup. "After all, soon it'll be too cold to go up to the mountain at all."

Fenton stopped in his tracks.

"Too cold?" he repeated. "What do you mean?"

"The digging season'll be over soon," said his father. "In fact, we're lucky we've been able to dig as long as we have."

"Oh, you mean because it's been so warm this year?" said Willy.

"That's right," said Mr. Rumplemayer. "One of the mildest autumns on record for this area, I've heard. Even so, I'd say we've probably only got a couple of weeks left to work outside. Then we'll have to stop until spring."

Fenton couldn't believe his ears. He was a little embarrassed to admit it, but somehow he hadn't really thought about what would happen out at the dig site once it got cold. He supposed that what his father had said made sense, but he still hated the idea that there might not be any more digging for fossils at Sleeping Bear once winter came.

"Do we really have to stop digging?" he asked. "I mean, couldn't we just wear lots of warm clothes?"

"I don't think so, son," said Mr. Rumplemayer. "It gets awfully cold up in the mountains in the winter. The ground'll be frozen solid."

"Not only that, but Sleeping Bear'll be covered with snow," added Willy. "It usually is by now. And sometimes the road up there gets completely blocked."

"Oh," said Fenton, feeling a wave of disappointment wash over him. He'd been visiting the dig site ever since the summer, when he had first moved to Morgan, and it was just about his favorite place in the whole world. He couldn't believe that soon he wouldn't be able to go there at all. "Too bad it just can't stay warm," he said wistfully, climbing into the back of the pickup.

"Yeah, I know," said Willy, scrambling in after him. "But winter's fun too. When it snows, everybody goes sledding on the hill behind the school. And we can go skating on the pond on Maggie's ranch."

"Yeah, I guess," said Fenton as the truck pulled out of the driveway.

Skating on a pond did sound kind of fun. In New York, the only places to go ice skating had been ice rinks. But still, ice skating was definitely no substitute for the dig site.

"Hey, I almost forgot to tell you," said Willy as they

bounced up Sleeping Bear Mountain Road. "I think there's something really weird going on at the shack."

"What do you mean?" asked Fenton, scratching Owen behind the ears.

"Well," said Willy, "when I went out there this morning, it seemed like some stuff had been moved around."

"Moved around?" Fenton repeated. "Like what kind of stuff?"

"One of the crates was turned on its side," said Willy. "And one of my comic books wasn't where I'd left it."

Just then the truck pulled to a stop in front of the big gates of the Carr Ranch, where Maggie was waiting.

"That does sound strange," Fenton said to Willy. "But you probably just left things that way yourself and forgot about it."

"Hi, you guys," said Maggie, climbing into the truck with them.

"No I didn't, Fenton," insisted Willy. "I'm sure of it."

"Sure of what?" asked Maggie as the truck took off again toward the mountain.

"Oh, Willy was just saying that some stuff in the shack wasn't where he thought he'd put it," explained Fenton.

"What's missing?" asked Maggie.

"Nothing's *missing*," said Willy. "But a crate was tipped over, and a comic book was moved. Yesterday, when we left to go play Ping-Pong, I put the *Ghostimonials* comic book I was reading on a stack in the corner. But when I stopped by there this afternoon, I found it on top of a crate that had been turned on its side."

"So?" said Maggie. "You must not have put it where you thought you did, that's all."

"Yeah," said Fenton. "You probably just forgot."

Willy shook his head. "I know I put it on the stack in the corner; I remember it. That's where I keep all my *Ghostimonials*. And that crate definitely wasn't tipped over, either."

"Well, you must be remembering wrong or something," said Maggie. "Anyway, what's the big deal? You found the comic book, right?"

"Yeah, but that's not the point," said Willy. "The point is, don't you think it's kind of strange that it happened to be *that* comic book, the one with the ghost stories in it, that was mysteriously moved?"

Maggie groaned. "Oh, Willy, don't tell me you're still on that ghost kick."

"Really," said Fenton. "I think you'd better stop reading those things; they're starting to go to your head."

"Look," said Willy, "I'm not saying it was definitely a ghost. I'm just saying it's pretty strange. But a lot of people do think that when you talk about ghosts, they're more likely to come around."

"What do you mean?" asked Fenton. "I've never heard that."

"Oh sure," said Willy. "There are a bunch of stories like

that in *Ghostimonials.*" He paused. "They say it especially happens when there are people around talking about how they don't believe in ghosts."

"Oh, I'm so scared,"said Maggie jokingly.

"Hey, you have to admit, it is pretty weird, a comic book and a crate just moving *themselves* like that," said Willy. "Who knows, maybe this is the evidence you guys were looking for."

"Sorry, Willy," said Fenton, "but it'd take a lot more than a knocked-over crate and a misplaced comic to convince me that there's a ghost in the shack."

"Yeah," said Maggie, grinning. "Call us when it starts playing the piano, okay?"

A few minutes later, they arrived at the dig site, near the top of the mountain. Mr. Rumplemayer parked next to the other two green pickups, a short distance from the trailer that the paleontologists used as an office and supply house.

Fenton could see Charlie Smalls and Lily Martin, the two other members of the dig team, in the distance. They were walking very slowly, in different directions, both looking intently down at the ground in front of them. To anyone who wasn't familiar with fossil-hunting, the scene would have looked very peculiar: two people inching away from each other, apparently studying their shoes. But to Fenton it made all the sense in the world. In fact, he couldn't wait to join them.

Fenton, Maggie, and Willy climbed out of the back of the

truck, followed by Owen. Mr. Rumplemayer stepped out of the truck's cab, and they all walked over to Charlie and Professor Martin.

"Still no luck, eh?" said Mr. Rumplemayer.

"No," sighed Professor Martin. "Nothing yet."

Charlie grinned. "I see you brought out some reinforcements, though," he said, indicating Fenton, Maggie, and Willy.

"That's right," said Fenton. "We're here to help out."

"Well, good," said Charlie. "The chances of finding something will definitely be better with six of us looking."

Owen barked once.

"Uh—make that seven of us," said Charlie, laughing. "Sorry about that, Owen."

Fenton laughed too. But he couldn't help hoping that Charlie was right, and that they would make a fossil find that day. Now that he knew their time on the mountain was limited, it seemed more important than ever to locate the next excavation site quickly.

"I suppose the best thing to do is split up," said Mr. Rumplemayer. "That way each of us can search a different area."

"Okay," said Fenton.

"But how will we know for sure if we've found a fossil?" asked Willy, looking a little worried. "I mean, sometimes they're kind of hard to recognize, right?"

"Just give a holler if you find anything unusual at all," said Charlie. "Then one of us will be over to check it out."

"If you want, you can look with me, Willy," Maggie offered. "That way we can kind of help each other."

"Okay, sure," said Willy.

"I guess Owen and I will be a team too," said Fenton, reaching down to stroke the dog's head.

Fenton's father assigned them each an area to work in, and everyone took off. Fenton's section began behind the paleontologists' trailer, and he decided to cover the area in a series of rows, walking first in one direction, and then back again, making sure not to miss a single square foot of land.

Fenton walked along slowly, with Owen creeping beside him, sniffing the ground. As Fenton searched the dry, pebbly ground at his feet, he thought about all the things that had to happen to create a successful fossil find.

First of all, when the dinosaur died, back in the Mesozoic, its body had to be covered up fairly quickly. It was all right if the animal's flesh had started to decompose, but if the bones disintegrated before something came along to preserve them, they would never have a chance to be fossilized. There were several ways the bones could be preserved. Sometimes, whatever had killed the dinosaur, say a volcano or a collapsing sand dune, could also fossilize it. In other cases, the dead animal's body could be washed into a river, lake, or ocean, where the sediment at the bottom would cover and preserve it.

Then, after being preserved for millions of years, the fossil had to become at least partially exposed. Usually this happened through erosion, which was when weather ate away at the rock it was buried in, but the natural shifting of the ground could help too, by pushing a fossil up toward the surface. Finally, someone had to come along and notice the exposed fossil before erosion caused it, too, to crumble and disappear. All in all, it was a pretty big lineup of events, and if just one of them went wrong, the whole process was ruined. No wonder only about a few thousand good dinosaur skeletons had ever been found, even though millions upon millions of dinosaurs had lived in the Mesozoic.

Fenton continued walking, peering carefully down at the ground in front of him. Willy had been right; sometimes it *was* hard to recognize a fossil when you saw one. This was partly because fossils were often similar in color to the rock or ground that surrounded them. And it didn't help that what you were looking for could be anything from a complete skeleton embedded in a huge boulder to a tiny chip of bone lying loose in the dirt. In fact, sometimes fossils weren't bones at all. Footprints, claws, teeth, and even dinosaur droppings counted as fossils.

Fenton reached the back of the trailer and got ready to do his next pass over the area of land. As he did, he walked up

onto a slight rise in the ground behind the trailer and noticed dark clouds gathering in the sky. He hoped it wasn't going to rain. That would mean the end of fossil hunting for the day.

Fenton looked down at the ground again as he prepared to turn around and start his next row. As he did, he noticed that the rise behind the trailer was covered with rocks and gravel, and mixed in here and there were some interesting-looking, thin, hard, grayish chips.

Fenton bent down to look closer, wondering what the chips could be. They definitely didn't look like any pieces of bone he'd ever seen. Maybe they were fragments of some kind of rock. He reached down and picked one up.

The piece in his hand was about the size of a quarter. Its edges were jagged, and the surface was pebbly on one side and smooth on the other. It was very slightly curved, almost as if it had once been part of something round.

Then Fenton had a flash; if what he was thinking was true, this could be an amazing find!

He looked around wildly. As he did, he saw that, in fact, the rise behind the trailer was actually a mound, an almost perfect circle about four feet across.

Suddenly Fenton knew exactly what he was looking at.

"Dad! Charlie! Everyone! Come quick!" he yelled. "I think I just discovered a nest!"

3

"What do you think?" asked Professor Martin as Mr. Rumplemayer examined one of the small gray fragments in his hand.

"It does look like eggshell," said Fenton's father, shaking his head in amazement. His eyes scanned the surface of the mound. "And there appear to be quite a few pieces of it around."

"Wow," said Willy appreciatively. "Real dinosaur eggs. That's so cool."

Charlie chuckled. "And to think we were sitting right in front of it all this time."

"Astounding," agreed Professor Martin. "Right under our noses."

Fenton beamed. If this was in fact a dinosaur nest, it would probably turn out to be a pretty important discovery.

"Do you think it is a nest, Dad?" he asked.

"It does look as though it is," said Mr. Rumplemayer. He pointed out the perimeter of the mound with his finger. "It seems like the dinosaur hollowed out a round ditch right here to lay her eggs in."

"Hollowed out?" said Willy. "But then shouldn't it be a hole? Why does it look like a hill?"

"When the dinosaur dug out the hole, it would have created a rim of dirt around the edge of the nest," explained Charlie. "Then, later on, when the nest was fossilized, the dirt would have filled it right up and made this mound."

"I get it," said Maggie. "Kind of like a big overflowing bowl."

"Exactly," said Charlie.

"Well," said Mr. Rumplemayer, "I guess the first thing we'd better do is move this trailer over some so we can get to the mound."

"Yes," said Professor Martin, glancing up at the sky. "And we should probably move quickly. Those clouds overhead look quite menacing."

Finally, a little later, the trailer had been moved. As his father and the team repositioned the trailer nearby, Fenton bent down eagerly to examine the mound.

"Oh wow," he said, reaching down to scoop up a handful of the surface gravel. "This is great!"

There was no doubt about it; it was already a pretty impressive find. And who knew what lay buried beneath the surface of the mound? Fenton couldn't wait to get the digging tools and start.

He looked up toward the trailer to call to his father.

But just as he opened his mouth, a great big fat snowflake fell right into it.

Later that evening, while his father made his way down the aisles of the Morgan Market, Fenton stood in front of the dairy case, looking at the cartons of eggs.

It was amazing to think that the small white eggs in the pink Styrofoam cartons in front of him were actually related to the fragments of dinosaur eggshell that were out at the dig site, under the tarp that the dig team had put down to protect the site from the snow. But after all, Fenton reminded himself, most scientists agree that birds are the closest living relatives of dinosaurs.

Fenton shivered a little, partly from the refrigerated air of the dairy case, and partly from excitement. For what seemed like the hundredth time that day, he wondered what kind of dinosaur had made the nest.

If only it hadn't started snowing, and they'd been able to dig. Why, at this very moment there could be hundreds of pieces of dinosaur eggshell just waiting to be found.

And that might not be all. Many paleontologists believed that dinosaurs took care of the babies in their nests for a while after they were hatched, which meant there was a chance there could be some baby dinosaur bones buried in the mound as well.

Or, if the eggs had become fossilized before they hatched, there might be some dinosaur embryos that had been fossilized. Either way, they'd be able to tell what kind of dinosaur had built the nest.

"Fenton," said his father, poking his head around a stack of cans, "what do you think we should have tonight—hamburgers or spaghetti?"

"Spaghetti," Fenton answered right away.

Spaghetti was Fenton's favorite dish. His mother used to make it with a special homemade tomato sauce in New York all the time, and not long after they had moved to Morgan, Fenton and his father had learned to follow her recipe.

Fenton decided to go outside to the old-fashioned gumball machine outside the market.

"Dad," he called to his father, "I'll be out front."

"All right," his father answered. "See you out there in a minute or two."

Fishing in his pockets for change, Fenton made his way out of the store to the concrete platform in front of the building. The gumball machine that was out there was older than any Fenton had ever seen in New York. And less expensive, too; it cost only a penny for a gumball.

Trouble was, all Fenton had in his pockets were two nickels

and a quarter. Gee, thought Fenton, laughing a little to himself, I guess cheaper isn't always better after all.

He sat down on the edge of the platform and looked around. The snow had stopped, and a thin layer of it covered the ground. The sun was just beginning to set, and the sky glowed pale purple beyond the mountains in the distance. Fenton saw a light go on in the back room of the Wadsworth Museum of Rocks and Other Natural Curios down the street. The museum was run by old Mrs. Wadsworth, who lived there, also. In addition to rocks, Mrs. Wadsworth collected and displayed animal skins, teeth, bones, feathers, birds' nests, and any other interesting natural artifact she could find. Fenton had visited the museum soon after arriving in Wyoming, and it was one of his favorite places in Morgan.

Just then Fenton thought he heard harmonica music coming from behind the store. It was a slow, sad-sounding song that Fenton didn't recognize. He hopped down the two concrete steps to the gravel parking lot and made his way around the side of the concrete building. As he headed toward the back of the store, he could hear, over the crunching of his feet in the gravel, the song coming to an end.

But when Fenton turned the corner, no one was there. He looked around, but all he could see were a few metal garbage cans, some empty cardboard boxes, and the trees beyond the store.

That's strange, he thought. But before he had time to think about it too much, he heard another sound. It was his father, calling his name.

"Fenton! Fenton, where are you?"

"Right here," Fenton called back.

He hurried around to the front of the building, where his father was standing by the green truck in the dirt parking lot, with three bags of groceries in his arms and his car keys dangling from one finger.

"I thought you said you were going to be out front," said his father, sounding a little exasperated.

"Sorry, Dad," said Fenton. "It was just that—"

"Here, help me out a little with these, would you, son?"

"Sure, of course, Dad," said Fenton, taking one of the bags. He opened the door to the pickup with his free hand, and he and his father slipped the grocery bags into the space behind the front seat.

Fenton slid into the passenger side. "Hey Dad, can I ask you something?"

"Certainly, Fenton," said his father. "What is it?"

"When you came out of the store, did you hear music?"

"Music? Why no, I don't think so," answered his father. "Now listen, I think we may have to make some adjustments in Mom's recipe, because they were out of pureed tomatoes. But I did get some regular ones, so I suppose we can puree them ourselves. Oh, and I also picked up some hamburger meat after all, so we can make meatballs if we want."

"Mmm, meatballs, great," said Fenton, feeling his stomach growl. All of a sudden, the harmonica music was the furthest thing from his mind. And he wasn't doing much thinking about the dinosaur eggs anymore either. In fact, right now the only thing Fenton seemed to be able to concentrate on at all was dinner.

4

"Now, this here is the way to do it," Charlie instructed.

It was Monday, and Fenton, Maggie, and Willy had bicycled out to the dig site after school. They were standing with Charlie and Mr. Rumplemayer on top of the mound. A few feet away, Professor Martin was busy chipping at the rock at the edge of the mound, trying to expose more of what the paleontologists thought might be the nest's original shape.

Fenton, Willy, and Maggie watched as Charlie scooped up a trowelful of dirt and carried it over to a large, flat, wooden box nearby. He dumped the dirt into the box, which had a screened bottom, and gently shook it. The dirt and finer pieces of gravel fell through to the ground, leaving the larger rocks and other particles inside the box.

"Here we go," said Charlie, peering into the box. "Looks like we've got ourselves a piece right here."

"You mean a piece of egg?" said Willy eagerly.

"That's right," Charlie answered. He took the triangular gray shard carefully between his thumb and forefinger and put it into the red plastic tray on the ground nearby.

"So, any pieces you kids find over here go in the tray," said Mr. Rumplemayer.

"Okay," said Fenton.

Maggie looked dubiously at the piece of eggshell in the tray. "Are you really going to be able to put all these bits back together to see what the eggs looked like?" she asked. "Some of them are kind of small."

"Well, we can certainly try," said Fenton's father. "But it won't be easy."

"You can say that again," Charlie said. He chuckled. "Good thing I like jigsaw puzzles, 'cause this sure is going to be a tough one."

"Once you get the eggs back together, will you know what kind of dinosaur laid them?" asked Willy.

"Not necessarily," said Mr. Rumplemayer. "But we will be able to compare them to other known dinosaur eggs and get some ideas. Of course, there's always the chance we may find some other clue to the dinosaur's identity."

"You mean like bones from some of the babies, right?" said Fenton.

"Well, of course, that would be an ideal way to tell what kind of dinosaur built the nest," said his father. "But we may not be that lucky."

Just then Professor Martin stood up from her digging.

"All right, I'd say we have ourselves some kind of a nest here," she said.

"Wonderful. What have you found?" asked Fenton's father.

"Well," she said, indicating the exposed ridge that bordered the mound, "all this here appears to be sandstone."

Fenton nodded. That made sense. The dinosaur had probably dug out the nest on the sandy bank of a river or inland sea.

"And directly underneath the surface dirt and gravel, the mound itself is mudstone," she said.

"So it's like the bowl of the nest is made of sandstone, and the mudstone is what's filling it up," said Maggie.

"That's right," said Professor Martin. "Which means there's a pretty good chance we'll find some eggshells embedded in the mudstone and the sandstone under it, as well as mixed with the gravel on top."

"Well, then, let's get started," said Mr. Rumplemayer. "Why don't you kids get to work on sifting through that gravel the way Charlie showed you. Meanwhile, we'll see how much more of this mudstone we can chip away."

"Okay, Dad," said Fenton as his father and Charlie stepped over to where Professor Martin was working.

Just then Willy bent down to the ground and picked something up.

"Wow," he said. "What a cool rock. It almost looks like there's a face in it."

Fenton looked down at the flat brown rock with black markings. "A face?"

"Yeah," said Willy pointing. "Look. Here are the eyes, and

here's the nose, and this part down here is like a mouth."

"Oh, yeah," said Fenton, making it out.

"I guess those markings do kind of look like a face," agreed Maggie.

"I like it," said Willy. "Maybe I'll keep it."

"You should probably make sure it's okay," said Maggie. "You know, that it's not important or anything."

"I doubt it is," said Fenton. "It just looks like a regular old rock to me. But I guess we might as well check just in case." He turned to Charlie. "Hey Charlie, can you take a look at this?"

"Sure," said Charlie, standing up. "What've you got?"

"I think it's just a rock," said Fenton. "But Willy wants to make sure before he takes it."

Charlie took the rock in his hand and examined it. "Actually, it looks like a piece of petrified wood to me. And hey, look at that; it's even got a tree ghost in it."

"A tree ghost?" Fenton repeated. "What are you talking about?"

"Don't you see that face?" said Charlie.

"Well, sure," said Fenton, "but . . ."

"That's the tree ghost," said Charlie. "My grandma always used to say that anytime you cut a piece of wood from a tree and saw a face like that, it was a tree ghost. So I guess it works for petrified wood, too. It's supposed to be good luck."

"Wow," said Willy. "That's cool." He put the rock in his jacket pocket.

"Oh, come on," said Fenton. "You don't actually believe that, do you, Charlie?"

"Yeah," said Maggie. "It's totally unscientific."

"Maybe so," said Charlie with a grin. "But all I know is my grandma never lied to me."

Fenton was kind of surprised. Charlie was a scientist. He couldn't possibly believe a story like that, could he?

"Okay, listen, you guys," said Maggie. "I have an idea. Let's divide things up. You know, one of us will scoop the gravel, and the other two can shake it through the screen and pick out the fossils. We could even take turns."

"All right," said Fenton. "Sounds good to me."

"I'll start scooping," volunteered Willy.

Fenton and Maggie took hold of either side of the box, and Willy shoveled a couple of trowelfuls of dirt and gravel into it.

"Look," said Maggie, pointing into the box. "That's one right there, isn't it?"

Fenton picked up the small gray piece.

"Yeah, I think so," he said. "Let's put it in the tray."

"Hey," said Willy, putting the next trowelful of dirt into the box, "how do you think the shells got broken up like this?"

"Well," said Fenton as he and Maggie shook the dirt through the screen, "if the dinosaurs hatched before the eggs became fossils, the babies themselves may have done it."

"You mean when they broke out of the eggs," said Maggie.

"Right," said Fenton. "And then afterward by walking

around on the pieces."

"I'm surprised they didn't break when the mother sat on them," said Willy. "After all, she was probably a big dinosaur, and they must have been pretty delicate."

"Actually, scientists think that a lot of dinosaurs probably didn't sit on their eggs," said Fenton. "So she may have just covered them up with some leaves and stuff to keep them warm while she was waiting for them to hatch."

"Oh," said Willy. "I guess that makes sense."

"I read that at least some dinosaurs were probably pretty good parents," said Maggie. "You know, that they took care of their babies in the nests."

"Yeah," said Fenton. "There's even one dinosaur, the maiasaur, whose name means 'good mother lizard.'"

"Wow," said Willy. "I never thought about dinosaur names meaning things."

"But they all do," said Fenton. "Like tyrannosaurus means 'ruler lizard,' and velociraptor means 'swift robber.' The word dinosaur itself means 'terrible lizard.' Anytime someone discovers a new dinosaur, that person gets to name it."

"Cool," said Willy. "I guess if I discovered a new dinosaur, I'd name it 'willysaurus.'" They laughed.

As the afternoon wore on, Mr. Rumplemayer and the others continued digging away at the mudstone, working to uncover whatever fossils might be embedded in it and to expose as much of the original shape of the nest as possible.

Meanwhile, the tray Fenton, Maggie, and Willy were working on began to fill with pieces of eggshell. The smallest of them were the size of a quarter, and the largest were almost as big as Fenton's palm.

As the sun went behind the mountain and the air grew cooler, Fenton shivered a little. He thought about what his father had said about the digging season being over soon. It was a good thing they had discovered the nest and its contents before the ground froze.

"Well," said his father, standing up and stretching a little. "Maybe it's time to call it quits."

"That sounds fine," agreed Professor Martin, putting down her tool. "I'd say we've done enough digging for one day."

"Oh, I don't know about that," said Charlie, looking up with a smile. "I think I have one more thing over here that just might be worth digging up before we go."

5

"Boy, your dad and the others sure did seem happy about that bone Charlie found yesterday," said Willy as he, Fenton, and Maggie walked through the school yard after school the next day.

"Actually, it was just a piece of a bone," said Fenton. "They think it's from a femur."

"A femur, that's a leg bone, right?" said Maggie, adjusting her backpack on her shoulder.

"Yeah," said Fenton. "And judging from the size of this piece, it must have been from a pretty small leg. Like from a baby, or maybe even an embryo that was still in the egg when it was fossilized."

"But they don't know what *kind* of baby dinosaur it was from?" asked Willy.

Fenton shook his head. "No, they can't tell just from this piece. But if there's one piece, chances are there'll be more of them. That's why they were so excited about it."

"I get it," said Willy.

"Hey, look," said Maggie as they approached the schoolyard gate. "There's Owen."

Sure enough, Owen was sitting just outside the gate, ears cocked and tail wagging. As soon as he saw Fenton, he let out a bark.

"That's amazing," said Willy. "He met you after school last week once too, didn't he?"

"That's right," said Fenton proudly.

Lately Fenton had been letting Owen out of the house in the mornings before leaving for school. At first he'd been kind of nervous about it, but the dog always seemed to return home in time for dinner. And now he'd started meeting Fenton after school sometimes.

Fenton shook his head. Owen was definitely an amazing dog. He'd always seemed to understand anything Fenton said to him, and now it was almost as if he could tell time, too!

"Good boy, Owen," said Fenton, bending down and letting the dog lick his face. "Hey, fella, how're you doing?"

"Hi, Owen," said Willy, patting him on the head. "Hey, listen, you guys. Do you want to head over to Mrs. Wadsworth's with me?"

"Sure," said Fenton, standing up.

It had been a while since he had visited Mrs. Wadsworth. It was always fun to go and see what new specimens she had.

"Okay," said Maggie. "As long as we don't spend too much time there. I have to get back to the ranch and take care of Pepper."

Pepper was Maggie's horse. Maggie was the only person Fenton had ever known who had her own horse as a pet.

"We don't have to stay long," said Willy. "I just thought I'd go over there and give her that piece of petrified wood I found at the dig site yesterday."

"Oh, you mean the one with the *tree ghost*?" said Maggie, rolling her eyes a little. "Just kidding. Listen, though, I thought that was supposed to be good luck, Willy. How come you're not keeping it for yourself?"

Willy shrugged. "I don't know. I guess I just got to thinking that Mrs. Wadsworth might like to have it for the museum."

"That's cool," said Fenton.

As far as Fenton was concerned, it was always a good idea to give something to a museum. Somehow it just never seemed right to him that there were private collectors who kept even things like important dinosaur finds to themselves.

But when they got to Mrs. Wadsworth's a few minutes later, the door to the little red building was locked, and there was a small handwritten note taped up outside.

> Gone out specimen hunting.
> Be back at sunset.

"Oh, well," said Willy. "I guess I'll have to come back some other time."

He reached into his pocket, took out the small piece of petrified wood, and tossed it into the air once, catching it in the palm of his hand. As he did, Owen leapt up and barked, trying to get at it.

"No, boy, that's not for you," said Fenton, laughing. "Down, Owen, down. Here, let me get you a stick." He looked around the dirt parking lot.

"How about over there," suggested Maggie, pointing at Cregg's lumberyard, across the street. A pile of scrap wood lay outside the gate. "I bet there's a piece the right size for him in that heap."

Fenton trotted across the street and picked up a piece of two-by-two from the pile.

"Here you go, Owen," he said, holding the wood above his head.

Owen bounded across the street and began barking wildly.

Fenton hurled the wood into the empty field next door. "Fetch!"

"Aw, that was kind of mean," said Maggie, crossing the street with Willy toward Fenton. "The grass there's so high. How's he going to find it?"

"No problem," said Fenton. "Watch."

Fenton was always amazed at how good Owen was at fetching. It was almost as if he had some kind of radar.

Sure enough, moments later, Owen came bounding back with the two-by-two in his mouth.

"Good boy," said Fenton, taking the stick from Owen and rubbing the dog's head. "Good dog."

"Okay, I'm impressed," said Maggie.

"Let me try now," said Willy.

Fenton held the piece of wood out, and Owen took it in his mouth.

"Go on, Owen. Bring it to Willy," said Fenton. "Bring Willy the stick."

Owen paused just a moment, cocking his ears. Then he took off toward Willy, waving the piece of wood happily.

"That dog is amazing," said Maggie as Willy took the two-by-two from Owen. "He understands every word you say, Fen."

"Oh, yeah?" said an angry-sounding voice behind them. "Well, does he understand the meaning of the words 'private property'?"

Fenton turned around. There, standing right in front of him, his hands folded across his chest and an angry look on his face, was Buster Cregg. Buster, whose uncle owned the lumberyard, was in Fenton and Maggie's class at school. Buster and Fenton definitely did not get along. In fact, Buster was the closest thing to an enemy Fenton had ever had.

Standing a little bit behind Buster were three of his friends, Matt Lewis, Jen Wilcox, and Jason Nichols. The four of them must have been behind the lumberyard, in the storage building that they used as a clubhouse, Fenton realized.

"So you're the one," Buster went on, glaring at Fenton. "Looks like I finally caught you red-handed."

"Uh, what do you mean?" asked Fenton.

"*Uh, what do you mean?*" Buster mimicked. Matt and Jen snickered behind him, and Jason looked down at the ground. "Don't play dumb with me, Oddball."

Fenton flinched. He hated the way Buster always called him "Oddball."

"This wood doesn't belong to you, and you know it," Buster went on. "You're just lucky I don't tell my uncle."

"Oh, come on," said Maggie disdainfully. "It's just a piece from the scrap heap. What's your problem, *Wendell*?"

Fenton cringed a little. Buster hated to be called by his real name as much as Fenton hated to be called Oddball. But that never stopped Maggie. She had a way of saying exactly what would get herself, and whoever happened to be with her, into trouble.

Fenton could see Buster's face reddening.

"Look, I was just borrowing it for a minute," said Fenton. He reached for Owen's collar and took the piece of wood from his mouth. "There," he said, tossing it back onto the pile. "See? No harm done. Come on, guys, let's go."

He beckoned to Maggie and Willy and started back down the road.

"Yeah, well, I'd watch out if I were you," Buster called after them. "It looks to me like you've *borrowed* a little too much wood already as it is."

"Wow, what was that all about?" said Willy, once they were out of earshot.

"Beats me," said Fenton.

"That Buster is such a pain," said Maggie.

"I think he's just plain crazy," said Willy. "What was all that stuff about borrowing too much wood?"

"Who knows?" said Fenton.

And who cares, he added to himself. What difference did it make what happened to wood that had already been scrapped?

6

"Wow," said Fenton, climbing off his bicycle at the dig site two days later. "Look at all this!"

Mr. Rumplemayer, who was crouched on the excavation site, glanced up from his digging.

"Oh, hello, son," he said. His gaze moved quickly over the mound. "Yes, we've been doing quite a lot of work up here."

"I'll say," said Fenton, looking at the mound with excitement.

Most of the surface gravel that he, Maggie, and Willy had been going through was cleared away now, and a large part of the mudstone mound beneath it had been excavated as well. One entire section of the nest's original shape was now visible, including a portion of the slightly raised ridge of sandstone around its perimeter.

"We've been removing a lot of the mudstone in chunks," his father explained. "And then using acid to dissolve the rock and loosen up any fossils that might be inside."

"I see," said Fenton. "Are the fossils all eggshells, or have you found any more bones?"

"Well, so far mostly eggshells," his father answered. "But it does look as if there may be some bone in a few of the chunks of mudstone we removed from further down in the mound. Charlie and Professor Martin are working on that right now, over in the trailer."

"What should I do?" asked Fenton eagerly. "Do you need me to help with the digging here?"

"That would be great, if you feel like it," said his father. He pointed to the other end of the exposed part of the nest's rim, opposite where he was working. "Maybe you could start over there. No one's really worked on that area yet. Just do what you can to dig up the mudstone and expose the sandstone."

"Okay," said Fenton.

He grabbed a pick from the red plastic tool chest on the ground and settled himself near the far end of the partly excavated perimeter of the nest. Turning his triceratops baseball cap backward on his head, he set to work, carefully chipping the darker mudstone away from the sandstone.

As he dug, Fenton couldn't help wondering again what type of dinosaur had made the nest. Maybe it had been one of the hadrosaurs—large, plant-eating dinosaurs from the Cretaceous. Lots of hadrosaur nests had been found in Montana, which was right next door to Wyoming.

Fenton tried to imagine the scene as it would have been back in the late Cretaceous, when hadrosaurs had lived. A large hadrosaur—a lambeosaur, or maybe a maiasaur—walked through the sand, her tail extended behind her, her delicately curved neck supporting her narrow head, and her eyes darting from side to side as she searched for a place to make her nest.

Once she had chosen the location, she began to dig in the sand, hollowing out a ditch. As she dug, the sand she removed from the nest piled up on its edges, forming a ridge that would help protect her eggs. Later, when the eggs hatched, the ridge might even help keep the babies in the nest, almost like a giant playpen.

Once she had dug her nest, the dinosaur laid her eggs and carefully covered them with leaves from nearby plants. And then she began her wait for the eggs to hatch. No one knew how long dinosaur eggs had to sit and incubate before they hatched; there was no way to tell from fossils. And, Fenton reminded himself, no one knew for sure yet whether the dinosaur eggs in this nest had ever hatched at all before becoming fossilized. If, for example, something had happened to the mother dinosaur and she wasn't there to care for the eggs anymore, keeping them covered with vegetation and protecting them from other animals, the baby dinosaur embryos might have perished before they ever had a chance to hatch.

As Fenton dug at the mudstone near the edge of the nest, he began to notice something interesting in the portion of the

sandstone ridge he was uncovering. There appeared to be the beginning of a narrow indentation of some kind pressed into the sandstone itself. He wondered what it was, and decided to concentrate his digging in that area to see how much of it he could uncover.

Just then Charlie came walking over from the trailer. In addition to his usual jeans and cowboy hat, he was wearing thick work gloves.

"Well, howdy, there, Fenton," he said. "Decided to come on up and give us a hand, eh?"

"Hi, Charlie," said Fenton, looking up from his digging.

For a moment he was tempted to point out the indentation in the sandstone that he was working to expose. But he decided it would probably be better to wait until he had uncovered more of it.

"So, tell me, how are things going back at the trailer, Charlie?" asked Fenton's father. "Have you and Professor Martin managed to come up with anything interesting yet?"

"Well, we do have a couple more pieces of bone, but not enough to tell for sure whose nest this was," Charlie answered. "But we have found quite a lot of eggshell." He tipped back his cowboy hat and scratched his chin. "You know, it's kind of interesting. For some reason, the pieces of shell from the bottom of the nest are turning out to be much tinier than the ones we found at the beginning, near the top."

"That's kind of weird," said Fenton. "I wonder why."

Charlie shrugged. "Who knows? Professor Martin's been working on piecing together a few of the larger chunks, though, so we may have an idea pretty soon of what the eggs actually looked like."

"Really?" said Fenton. He felt a little shiver of anticipation go up his spine. Suddenly he couldn't wait to see the eggs. "Hey, Dad," he said, "I'm going to go over to the trailer and have a look, okay?"

"Sure, son," answered Mr. Rumplemayer, looking intently back down at the area where he had been digging. "You go ahead. I'll probably be over in a few minutes. I think I may see something interesting here, and I just want to get it uncovered first."

Normally Fenton would have offered to stay and help his father work on whatever it was he was uncovering. But the idea of actually seeing one of the eggs reconstructed was just too exciting to wait another minute.

"You know, I think I'll head back over that way with you and take a look too," said Charlie. "Besides, I could use a soda about now."

Fenton and Charlie made their way over to the trailer's new location. When they got inside, they found Professor Martin sitting at the big table that the paleontologists used as a desk and worktable.

"Oh, hello there, Fenton," she said, looking up briefly from her work.

"Hi, Professor Martin," said Fenton. "I hear you're trying to put some of the egg pieces back together."

"Just like Humpty Dumpty," joked Charlie.

"Come have a look," Professor Martin said.

Fenton walked over to the table. Spread out on it were dozens of gray eggshell chips, each one numbered in white chalk. Several had been pieced together, enough to reconstruct almost one entire side of an egg.

Fenton peered intently at the egg. It was about five inches long and fairly narrow, with a point at one end. There were several chips missing from the reconstruction, and the pieces that had been fitted together were somewhat irregular, giving the egg a bumpy, cracked appearance. But there was no doubt about it: The object there on the table was an egg, suddenly just as real to Fenton as the eggs in their cartons at the Morgan Market.

"That's really incredible," said Fenton under his breath, still examining the egg in front of him.

"Yes, isn't it exciting?" said Professor Martin. "Seeing it pieced together like this makes it so much easier to imagine how the nest must have looked when it was filled with them."

"It sure does," agreed Charlie, reaching into the red cooler on the floor for a can of soda. "Now, if only we could get as clear an idea of what the little critters inside were like."

"Ah, yes," said Professor Martin. "So far the bone pieces we've found have been something of a disappointment. There are too few of them, and what we have are so tiny that we just can't make a positive identification."

Just then the door to the trailer burst open and Fenton's father hurried in, cradling something in his hands.

"Well, I think I've found it!" he said, a little out of breath. "I think I've found what we've been looking for."

"Really?" said Professor Martin. "You've got a good bone?"

"I certainly do," said Mr. Rumplemayer. "It was right down near the bottom of the nest."

He held out his hand. Sitting on his palm was a small fossil, still covered in places with bits of mudstone. Fenton leaned closer to get a better look.

At first Fenton couldn't quite figure out what it was. But then, suddenly, he recognized the shape of the piece of bone. The only reason he hadn't been able to place it at first, he realized, was that it was so much smaller than any he had ever seen.

There, sitting right in the palm of his father's hand, was a piece of bone. Fenton could just make out an upper jaw, complete with little teeth and the curve of a tiny beak. He could barely believe his eyes. But there was no doubt about it.

"It's a skull, right?" he said.

"That's right. And it looks as if it's got the beginning of a rostral bone," Fenton's father said, pointing to the tiny beak.

"That means it's a horned dinosaur," said Fenton.

"Well, I'll be," said Charlie. "A ceratopsian. Isn't that something!"

"It's really a marvelous specimen," agreed Mr. Rumplemayer, beaming. "And it appears to be from an embryo."

"How can you tell?" asked Fenton.

"Take a look at the teeth," said his father. "They're perfectly formed at the edges; it's clear they've never been used."

"Oh," said Fenton, nodding. That made sense. If the dinosaur had never been born, it obviously had never had a chance to use its teeth.

"Imagine that," said Charlie, shaking his head. "We're seeing a piece of this little guy just the way he must have been all curled up in his shell."

"Well," said Fenton's father, putting the bone down on the table. "I guess that settles the question of whether or not the eggs hatched before they were fossilized. From this, I'd say it looks like they never had a chance to."

Fenton looked from his father to Charlie. It was obvious in both of their faces how pleased they were with this find. His father's eyes were shining, and Charlie's face was flushed. And Fenton knew just how they felt. This little bone had answered a lot of questions. Now they knew that the nest had belonged to a ceratopsian and that the eggs had been unhatched.

The only person there who didn't seem to have anything to say at all was Professor Martin.

Fenton looked at her. For some reason she didn't seem nearly as excited as everyone else. In fact, if anything, she looked pretty upset. Her brow was furrowed, and her mouth was turned down at the corners.

And as Fenton's gaze moved from her face down to the reconstructed egg on the table in front of her, he realized exactly what was wrong.

7

"All right," said Maggie, taking a bite of her apple. "Let me get this straight. You're saying that the eggs were *smaller* than the dinosaur that was supposed to be in them?"

"Right," said Fenton dejectedly. He took a sip of his juice.

"But that doesn't make any sense," said Willy.

"I know," said Fenton. He shook his head. "No one can figure it out."

It was the following day, and Fenton, Maggie, and Willy were sitting in the Morgan Elementary cafeteria, eating lunch. Fenton had been thinking of nothing but the discovery at the dig site since the day before, but he hadn't been able to come up with a single possible explanation for the problem of the egg's size.

"But how can they tell for sure that the embryo's too big?" asked Maggie. "I thought you said they only found a piece of the skull."

"It's kind of obvious," said Fenton. "This piece alone is

practically two thirds the size of the egg. If you put it in the egg, there wouldn't be much room for the rest of the dinosaur."

"It's definitely pretty mysterious," said Maggie, biting into her apple again.

"Hey," said Willy, "speaking of mysterious, wait till I tell you the latest thing that happened out at the shack."

"Oh, no," said Maggie. "I hope this isn't going to be another one of your ghost stories."

"Just listen," said Willy. "I tell you, there's definitely something weird going on out there. This morning I went out before school to get a comic book, and I found the door wide open."

"So?" said Fenton.

"So, I always close it at night," said Willy.

"Oh, come on," said Maggie. "That's no big deal. It was probably just the wind or something."

Willy looked at them. "There hasn't been any wind for two days. Besides, how could the wind have undone the latch?"

"All right, then," said Fenton. "What about Jane?" Jane was Willy's little sister. "Maybe she was out there. You know how she's always following you around and stuff. Maybe she went out to look for you."

Willy shook his head. "No way. Jane's scared to walk through the woods by herself. She'd never go out to the shack."

"Okay," said Maggie. "So it wasn't the wind and it wasn't Jane. But that doesn't mean it was a ghost, Willy."

"Really," agreed Fenton. "There's got to be some sort of logical explanation for it."

Fenton knew that what he was saying was true. If you looked hard enough, there was a logical explanation for everything. Which meant there had to be one for what had been going on at the shack, and for the problem at the dig site, too. The trouble was, right now he had absolutely no idea what either of them could be.

"Okay, how about this, Fen?" said Maggie as the three of them headed over to Mrs. Wadsworth's later that afternoon. "Maybe the dinosaurs in the nest *weren't* embryos after all. Maybe they had already hatched and had some time to do a little growing before they were fossilized."

"Yeah," said Willy. "Then they could be bigger than their eggs, right?"

Fenton shook his head. "In order to do that much growing, they would have had to do some eating, too," he said. "But the teeth on the one we found looked like they'd never been used for anything."

"Okay," said Maggie as they approached the little red building. "Forget that idea, then."

"Oh, good," said Willy, pulling open the door to the rock museum. "It's open. I guess Mrs. Wadsworth must be here."

But when they got inside, Mrs. Wadsworth was nowhere in sight.

"She must be in the back," said Fenton.

Sure enough, a moment later Mrs. Wadsworth poked her head out from the door that led to the back room, where she lived.

"Why, hello, everyone!" she called out cheerfully. "How wonderful of you all to stop by for a visit. I'm a little busy at the moment, but I'll be with you in just a minute or two."

"Okay, Mrs. Wadsworth," said Willy as she disappeared behind the door again.

Fenton, Maggie, and Willie began to mill around the museum's front room, looking at the displays crammed onto every available surface.

"Look," said Maggie, reading one of Mrs. Wadsworth's hand-labeled cards. "These are eagle feathers."

"It says here that this rock has real flecks of gold in it," said Willy, examining another display.

Fenton gazed at the rocks and other specimens lining one of the shelves. Nestled between a pinkish rock and a snakeskin was a tiny brown bird. It was made out of wood, but it looked so real that it seemed as if it was about to fly off. He reached out to pick it up.

Just then Mrs. Wadsworth opened the door to the back again.

"All right then, Willy, Fenton, Maggie," she said. "Sorry to keep you all waiting like that. Do come in the back and have some oatmeal cookies. I have a fresh batch all made."

Fenton put the bird back on the shelf and followed the others to the back of the room. They walked into the little room where Mrs. Wadsworth lived and sat down at the table.

Mrs. Wadsworth put a baking sheet that was half-filled with cookies on the table.

"Help yourselves," she said. She went to the refrigerator, took out a carton of milk, and poured three glasses. "I'm sorry they're not too hot anymore."

"That's okay, Mrs. Wadsworth," said Fenton, taking a bite of a cookie. "They're really good."

"Why, thank you," she said. "Yes, people do seem to like them. It's my own special recipe, you know."

"Delicious," agreed Maggie.

"Gee," said Willy, cocking his head. "Do you hear that?"

Fenton listened. He could barely make out the sound of music, coming from somewhere outside.

"Hey," he said, suddenly realizing why the music sounded so familiar, "that's a harmonica, isn't it?"

"Hmmm, yes, I suppose it does sound like one," said Mrs. Wadsworth, pulling out a chair and joining them at the table. "So now, tell me, Fenton, how's everything out at Sleeping Bear Mountain? Have there been any interesting dinosaur discoveries lately?"

Fenton sighed. "Have there ever. A little *too* interesting, if you ask me."

Mrs. Wadsworth raised her eyebrows. "*Too* interesting? Now, how can that be?"

Fenton began to explain about the nest, the eggs, and the embryo, and soon he was so involved in what he was saying that he had forgotten all about the music. Mrs. Wadsworth listened sympathetically, clucking her tongue and shaking her head in disbelief.

"Well, that is quite a puzzle, isn't it," she said.

"It sure is," Maggie agreed. "It doesn't make any sense at all."

"Perhaps something else will turn up out at the site to help you sort it out," said Mrs. Wadsworth.

"I hope so," said Fenton.

"Hey," said Willy, "speaking of things turning up at the dig site, I brought you something." He fished around in his pocket and held his hand out for Mrs. Wadsworth to see. "It's petrified wood."

"It's perfectly lovely," exclaimed Mrs. Wadsworth, taking the piece from his hand. She peered at it through her half-moon spectacles. "Oh, and look—I think I even see a tree ghost in it."

Fenton and Maggie looked at each other.

"A *tree ghost*?" they said together.

"Well, sure," Mrs. Wadsworth went on. "Can't you see the face?"

Fenton shook his head in disbelief. It was starting to seem like everybody believed in this ghost stuff.

Mrs. Wadsworth smiled. "They say a tree ghost is supposed to be good luck, you know."

"Yeah," said Willy, looking at Fenton and Maggie triumphantly. "I do know."

8

Fenton looked out the window at the snow and then over at his father, who was sitting at his desk, still studying the papers he had been looking at all day.

It was Saturday, and it had been snowing lightly since morning. Fenton and his father had spent most of the day in the second-floor study of their house, going over the diagrams of the reconstructed eggshells and the skull piece and other bones from the nest. Several more ceratopsian bones had been found out at the dig site, and the paleontologists had been able to piece together one more egg. Normally this would have been very exciting, but everyone's spirits were down because there was still no way the ceratopsian embryos could ever have fit in either of the eggs.

In fact, if anything, the newly discovered fossils had just

confirmed how impossible the whole thing was. The bones had all been underdeveloped, some not even fully formed, which made it more certain than ever that they were from dinosaur embryos rather than from young hatchlings. The whole situation was more confusing than ever.

And Fenton, for one, couldn't stand to think about it anymore. He'd been sitting in this room since morning, going over every detail of the problem in his head. And he hadn't come up with a thing.

Owen paced across the room, his nails clicking on the wood floor. Fenton looked at his watch.

Thank goodness it was almost time to contact Max. Max Bellman was Fenton's friend in New York. Every Saturday evening they used the modems on their computers to play Treasure Quest, the computer game that Max had invented.

Just then the phone rang. Fenton hopped up from his seat and reached for it, relieved to have something to do.

"Hello?" he said.

"Hi, Fenton, honey!" said a faraway voice on the other end of the line. "How are you?"

"Mom?" said Fenton eagerly. "Is that you?"

Fenton saw his father look up from his work. Although his mother often wrote to them, and had even managed to send them a couple of letters by fax machine from India, she wasn't really able to call that often. She was spending a year traveling from dig site to dig site, and a lot of the places she ended up didn't even have telephones.

"I'm so glad I caught you," said Mrs. Rumplemayer. "I thought you might be out at the dig site with Dad."

"We didn't go today," said Fenton. "It's snowing."

"Oh, so you're both there, wonderful!" said his mother. "It's actually very early in the morning here, but this was the only chance I had to call. I have to catch a train in half an hour. So tell me, honey, how is everything?"

"Okay," he answered. "Dad and I have just been looking at some diagrams of a ceratopsian nest we discovered at Sleeping Bear."

"A nest—oh, how marvelous! Your father must be very pleased."

"Well, actually, there's a problem," Fenton explained. "You see, the ceratopsian embryos we found are too big to fit into the eggs."

"That's awfully peculiar," said his mother. "What does Dad think?"

"He's stumped," said Fenton. "Everybody is. It just doesn't make any sense at all."

"It certainly doesn't," she agreed. "Very strange. Listen, though, quickly, tell me how everything else is. I can't stay on too long, but I want to know how you're doing. How's school?"

"Fine," said Fenton. "Everything's fine. How's India?"

"Good," she answered, "but I miss you and Dad. The other day I met this very nice American couple, though. Somehow our luggage had gotten mixed up at the train station, and after we straightened it all out, they asked me to go to dinner with them. It was really very pleasant."

"You mean you went out to eat with people you didn't even know?" asked Fenton. Somehow it just didn't sound like something his mother would do.

"Yes, and I'm so glad I did," said his mother. "They are wonderful people, and I'm sure we'll keep in touch. You know, when they first asked me, I was going to say no, but then I thought, why not?" She laughed. "That's the problem with us New Yorkers; we can sometimes be too unfriendly and distrustful of people we don't know."

"Yeah, I guess you're right," said Fenton. "Here in Morgan, everybody's really friendly. People even say hello when they pass each other in town."

"That must be very nice," said his mother.

"Yeah," agreed Fenton.

"All right, then," said his mother. "Let me talk to your father now. And you take care, honey, okay?"

"Okay, Mom. Bye. Here's Dad."

Fenton handed the phone to his father. He sat down in front of the computer, turned it on, and activated the modem.

Max was waiting on the other end.

<HI FENTON. WHATS NU?>

]NOT 2 MUCH. ITS SNOWING. ALSO WE R HAVING
PROBLEMS OUT AT THE DIG SITE[

<WHATS GOING ON?>

]WE FOUND A DINO NEST WITH EGGSHELLS + PIECES
OF EMBRYOS, BUT WHEN WE PUT THE EGGS BACK 2-
GETHER THEY WERE 2 SMALL 2 FIT THE EMBRYOS[

 **<DID U USE A COMPUTER TO PUT THE EGGS BACK
2-GETHER, OR DO IT BY HAND?>**

]BY HAND[

<THAT COULD BE THE PROBLEM>

Fenton smiled to himself. One thing about Max, he almost always thought that a computer could do a job better than a human being could. In fact, one of his favorite sayings was "People make mistakes, computers don't." But Max had been to visit Fenton in Morgan recently, and it had actually seemed as if Max was starting to realize that there was quite a bit more to life than computers.

]WANT TO PLAY TQ NOW?[

Fenton keyed in.

came Max's response.

Before long, the boys were immersed in their game. One thing Fenton loved about playing Treasure Quest with Max was that it took his mind off everything else. Somehow it was really easy to lose himself in the world of explorers and caves and demons in the computer.

Just as they were about to start their third game, Fenton heard the telephone ring. He keyed in to Max to wait a minute, and reached over to pick it up. As he did, he noticed that his father wasn't in the room anymore. He also realized that it had stopped snowing.

"Hello?" he said into the receiver.

"Hi, Fenton it's me," said Willy.

"Oh, hi," said Fenton. "Listen, can I call you back in a little while? I'm on the computer with Max."

"Actually, it's kind of important," said Willy.

"Okay, sure, what is it?"

"I can't tell you now," said Willy. "You have to see it for yourself. Can you meet me at the shack in ten minutes?"

"Sure, I guess," said Fenton. "But what's up?"

"Just come to the shack and you'll see," said Willy. "Maggie's coming, too. I just called her."

"All right," said Fenton. "See you in ten."

He turned back to the computer.

]HEY MAX, I HAVE 2 GO NOW[

<NO PROBLEM. TALK 2 U NEXT WEEK>

]OK. BYE[

As Fenton turned off the computer, he wondered what it was that Willy wanted to show him. Whatever it was, it must be pretty important for both him and Maggie to have to see it right away.

Fenton slipped his feet into his sneakers and tied the laces. Owen looked up at him from the corner, wagging his tail hopefully.

"That's right, boy," said Fenton, standing up. "Come on, fella, we're going outside."

9

Ten minutes later Fenton walked through the woods between his house and Willy's, with Owen trotting behind him.

He found Willy standing out in front of the shack, a funny look on his face.

"Hi," said Fenton. "What's going on?"

"Just wait," said Willy as Owen ran over to the door of the shack and began sniffing around it. "As soon as Maggie gets here, I want to show you guys something."

A moment later they heard Maggie coming through the woods toward them, pushing branches out of her way.

"Boy," she said to Willy, "this better be important. It's cold out here." She looked at Owen, who had started to whine and paw at the door to the shack. "What's with him?"

"Beats me," said Fenton. "So, what's this important thing you want to show us, Willy?"

"All right, you guys," said Willy. "For days I've been trying to tell you that there's something funny going on out here, and you both keep saying there's a logical explanation."

"Sure," said Maggie. "That's right."

"Well," said Willy, "what I want to know now is, what's your explanation for this?"

He threw open the door to the shack, and Owen bounded inside and began sniffing all over the room.

Fenton followed Willy inside and looked in the direction Willy was pointing. There, in the corner, near one of the crates, was a little pile of what looked like wood shavings.

"Hey," said Fenton, moving closer. "What's that doing here?"

"Good question," said Willy.

"You mean these shavings aren't from you?" asked Maggie, peering down at them.

"Of course not," said Willy. "I came out here after the snow stopped and found them. Now do you guys believe me? There's definitely something very spooky going on out here."

"You're right, Willy," said Maggie, walking over to the window. "There is something weird going on."

"I agree," said Fenton. "Someone has definitely been here. And my guess is it wasn't a ghost, either. Just look at Owen; he's obviously picking up the scent of a person, a stranger."

"No, I don't think it's a ghost, either," said Maggie, peering out of the window. "That is, unless ghosts leave footprints."

"*Footprints?*" Willy repeated. "Where?"

"Right outside there, in the snow," said Maggie.

The three of them walked out of the shack. Outside the

window was the imprint of what looked like a large boot.

They looked at one another.

"Well, now there's no doubt about it," said Fenton. "Someone else has been in the shack."

"Yeah," said Willy, "and this isn't the only time, either. I'm telling you, stuff's been getting moved around here practically every night."

"Hmmm," said Fenton, thinking. "Are you sure these things are happening at night?"

"Pretty sure," said Willy. "I leave things one way at the end of the day, and when I come back the next morning, they're different. First it was the moved comic book and the knocked-over crate, and then the open door, and now this."

"Gee," said Maggie. "That's kind of creepy."

"It sure is," said Fenton. "And the way I see it, there's only one thing for us to do about it."

"What's that?" asked Willy.

"Catch whoever it is in the act," Fenton answered. "Now listen, here's my idea . . . ."

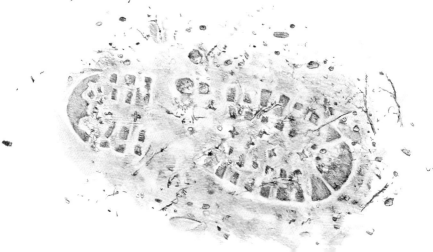

10

"Wow, it's cold," said Fenton, when the three of them met back at the shack later that night. "And dark." He was a little surprised, since the clear sky and full moon had illuminated the outside of the shack so well. "It's a good thing I remembered the flashlight." But when he switched it on, the beam of light that came out was very weak. "Gee, I guess maybe the battery's kind of low."

He sat down on the floor of the shack and wrapped his sleeping bag around himself.

"Wait till you guys see what *I* brought for us," said Maggie. She held up a large shopping bag.

"What's in there?" asked Willy.

"Leftovers," said Maggie with a grin. "I thought we might get hungry waiting here, so I asked Dina to pack up a few things to keep us from starving."

Dina was the cook for Maggie's family's ranch. She lived there and prepared meals for the ranch hands and the family.

Maggie began to unpack the bag. "Let's see. We have fried chicken and a thermos of hot cocoa and brownies."

"Wow, this looks great," said Fenton, picking up a piece of chicken.

Once again, he couldn't help feeling a little jealous of Maggie's cook. Especially tonight, since he and his father had split a can of chili for dinner.

"Hey, Maggie, what did you end up telling your mother about where you were going tonight?" asked Willy, spreading out his own sleeping bag.

"Well," said Maggie, pouring some cocoa into a cup, "I knew she'd never agree to let me camp out here, so I had to think of something to get out of the house. Luckily, Lila and Rob were going to the movies, so I just said I wanted to go too."

"Good thinking," said Fenton, biting into his chicken.

Lila was Maggie's older sister, and Rob was Lila's boyfriend. Lila and Maggie didn't get along that well, but their mother was always trying to get them to spend more time together. Maggie knew that anytime she told her mother she wanted to go somewhere with Lila, her mother would force Lila to take her along.

"So then I had Lila and Rob drop me off near your driveway, Fen," she said. "And I told them to pick me up there on their way back."

"And she agreed?" said Fenton, surprised. Somehow Lila

had never really struck him as the type to do favors for anybody, and especially not for her younger sister.

"Sure," said Maggie. "Are you kidding?" She laughed. "She was so relieved I wasn't coming to the movies that she would have agreed to anything. But this ghost or whatever it is had better show up by eleven o'clock, 'cause that's when I have to meet them to go home."

Willy looked a little worried. "You guys don't *really* think it could be a ghost, do you?"

Maggie shook her head in amazement.

"Willy, I thought you were the one who was so positive it was," she pointed out.

"I know," said Willy. "But now that we're here, I'm really starting to hope it isn't."

"Don't worry about it, Willy," said Fenton. "Even if ghosts did exist, which they don't, there's no way that whoever's been coming to the shack could be one. Remember, we saw a footprint."

"Yeah," said Maggie. "That mark in the snow was definitely left by a human being. Now, pass me those brownies."

Fifteen minutes later, they had finished eating.

"Whew," said Maggie, leaning back against the wall of the shack. "I'm stuffed."

"Me too," said Fenton.

They sat there in silence for a few moments.

"Too bad we only have one flashlight," said Willy, looking

around. "Otherwise we could all read comics while we wait."

"Well, someone could read out loud," suggested Maggie. She reached for the nearest comic book and picked up the flashlight, which flickered a little at her touch. "Oh, no, not *Ghostimonials!*" She put down the comic.

"Go on, read that one," said Willy. "I just got it, and I haven't even looked at it yet."

"This is so ridiculous," said Maggie, holding the flashlight up to the comic as she leafed through it. "Just listen to this: *'This true tale comes from prisoner #1769 at the Hallenworth Federal Prison. Prisoner #1769 is a murderer. But he is also somewhat unusual as inmates go, because although at first he was not found guilty of any crime at all, his experiences with the ghost of his victim terrified him so much that he eventually broke down and confessed to murder, and begged to be sent to jail.'"* She put down the comic book. "Oh, yeah, I'm so sure."

"Go on, read it," said Fenton, interested in spite of himself.

"All right," said Maggie, shrugging. "You asked for it. Here goes: *'Prisoner #1769 wasn't always a prisoner, of course. At one time, he was an average citizen, an accountant who worked for a big company, a man we shall call Mr. X.'"*

She looked up. "Mr. X. Give me a break.

"*'But one day at the office,'*" she went on, "*"'as Mr. X was going through the records, he came across a mistake. It was a big mistake. And it was a mistake that could make Mr. X a very rich man with just a stroke of his accounting pen. It seemed like the*

80

*perfect opportunity. No one had noticed the mistake but him . . .
or so he thought.'"*

"Oooh," said Willy. "So he stole the money."

"Yeah, I guess so," said Maggie. "It says, '*Mr. X quit his job
and used some of his newly found money to buy himself a place
in the country, a place with a pond and a big house surrounded
by woods. But soon after, he began receiving threatening letters
and phone calls. Someone back at the office had discovered what
he had done, and was blackmailing him, threatening to tell the
authorities.*

"'*Mr. X was frantic. He agreed to do whatever the caller
wanted in order not to be exposed. He was terrified of losing his
money and ending up in jail. But the blackmailer promised to
keep quiet only if he got half of the money that Mr. X had taken.*

"'*Desperate, Mr. X agreed to the terms. Arrangements were
made; the blackmailer would come to pick up the money at Mr.
X's country house. . . . But Mr. X had no intention of going
through with the plan. He had a plan of his own.*'"

"I get it," said Fenton. "He must have killed the guy."

"Hold on a second, let me read it to you," said Maggie. She
adjusted the flashlight, which had started to flicker. "'*At the
appointed time, the blackmailer, who turned out to be an office
clerk that Mr. X had known well, showed up. And when he did,
Mr. X was waiting for him . . . with a gun. After shooting him
once through the heart, Mr. X tied bricks to the man's head and
feet and dropped the body into the pond on his estate.*'"

"Yuck," said Willy.

"Yeah, look at the picture," said Maggie, shining the light on the comic book and showing it to them.

Fenton peered at the illustration in the dim light. It showed a close-up of a man's face, frozen into an expression of agony, with two large bricks tied to his neck and murky, green water in the background.

"*It was the perfect crime,*'" Maggie went on. "'*The black-mailer, fearful of being caught himself by the authorities, had told no one where he was going and hadn't left a trail of any kind. When it was discovered that he was missing, no one made any connection to Mr. X. In police records, it remained an unsolved case—no body and no suspects. It was the perfect crime. . . .*

"'*Or so Mr. X thought. But there was something he hadn't counted on, and that was that there was one person besides himself who knew what had really happened. And the ghost of that person, the clerk, doomed to rot away in his watery grave in the pond, could never rest until he had his revenge.*'" She looked up. "That *is* a little creepy, isn't it?

"'*The first night after the murder, as Mr. X was sitting in his house, he heard footsteps coming toward him through the woods. There was a wet, squelching, soggy sound with each step. Squelch . . . squelch . . . squelch . . .*'"

"Hold on a second," said Willy, interrupting her. "Did you hear that?"

"What?" said Fenton a little nervously.

"It sounded like someone was outside," said Willy.

"It was probably nothing," said Maggie.

"Yeah," said Fenton. "Go on."

Maggie started reading again. "'*Mr. X thought of the body in the pond, of how it would have begun to rot in the water, and his heart began to beat faster. Then, suddenly, the footsteps stopped and headed away from the house, back in the direction of the pond.*

"'*The following night, as Mr. X sat in his house, the footsteps began again. Squelch . . . squelch . . . squelch. This time they came closer before stopping and turning back.*

"'*Mr. X began to panic. He was terrified of seeing the soggy, rotting corpse of the dead clerk. And each night after dark, the footsteps would begin again, and each night they would come closer to the house than the night before. Finally, they were right outside his door . . . squelch . . squelch . . . sq—*'"

Fenton heard something outside. It sounded as if someone was coming through the woods, toward the shack.

"Hey, hold on," he said. "What was that?"

"I told you," said Willy, his voice trembling a little.

"Oh, my gosh," said Maggie, her eyes widening in the dim light. "Someone's coming!"

Just then the flashlight flickered and went off, and the door to the shack opened with a creak, revealing a tall figure silhouetted against the moonlit sky.

They all screamed at once.

11

"Oh, my!" exclaimed a voice. An electric lantern flickered on, illuminating the startled-looking face of an old man with thick white hair and a white beard. "How you scared me!"

"*We* scared *you?*" said Maggie incredulously.

"Why, yes," said the man. "Of course." He shook his finger at them. "Hiding out here in the dark and screaming at a person like that when he comes through the door. It's enough to scare the wits out of anyone!"

"Sorry," said Willy. "We didn't mean to scare you."

"That's quite all right," said the man. "No harm done."

"Who are you?" Fenton asked.

The man took a couple of steps inside and put down his lantern. He was wearing worn-looking pants, a thick brown quilted jacket, a black ski cap, and large work boots. He had a scruffy backpack over his shoulder and a harmonica hanging from a cord around his neck.

Fenton glanced around a little nervously. He had been so busy trying to convince Willy that there was no ghost that he hadn't stopped to think that whoever it was who *had* been in the shack could be dangerous.

"The name's Sam," said the man. "Sam Murrow. And I suppose you folks must be the ones who are using my shack."

"*Your* shack?" said Fenton, surprised.

"What do you mean?" said Maggie.

"This is *my* shack," said Willy.

"Yes, well, I imagine it is your shack now," said Sam, looking around. "Finders keepers, and all that. In that case, I hope you don't mind that I've been borrowing it a bit lately."

"I noticed that someone had been here," said Willy.

"But why?" asked Maggie. "What have you been doing here?"

"Mostly keeping out of the rain and the dark," said Sam. He glanced at a nearby stack of comics and grinned. "And catching up a little on my reading, too. I must say, I particularly enjoy the ones about the ghosts." He took off his backpack and looked around the room. "You know, it's amazing how little the place has changed in all the years since I first built it."

"Built it?" Willy repeated. "You mean you're actually the one who made this shack?"

"That's right," said Sam. "Made my mark down here on one of these boards, too." He squatted down and peered at a spot on the wall near the floor. "Here it is."

Fenton looked at the spot where the man was pointing. There, carved into a lower board on the wall, were the letters S.M., followed by the number 49.

"Wow," said Willy, examining the carving. "I can't believe I never noticed that before. S.M.—that's you, right?"

"Yep," said Sam, turning a crate on its side and sitting on it.

"But what's the forty-nine for?" asked Maggie.

"That's when I built the place," said Sam. "Back in 1949." He got a sad, faraway look in his eyes. "Spent most of that spring here, in fact."

"You mean you lived in here?" asked Fenton incredulously. The shack was so tiny, he couldn't imagine it ever having been anyone's home.

"Well, it was just supposed to be for the time being," said Sam. "While I was clearing some land back there in the woods to build a house. You see, I had just gotten married, and Emily, my wife, was waiting for me back in Cheyenne. As soon as I got the house finished, we were going to move in."

"So where's the house, then?" asked Maggie.

The sad look returned to his eyes.

"I never got to build it," he said. "Just as I was finishing clearing the land, I got the news that Emily had died. Pneumonia, the doctors said it was." He paused. "There just didn't seem any point in going on without her. So I decided to sell the property and pick up and leave, let the woods grow back and cover up the spot."

"But where did you go?" asked Willy.

Sam smiled. "You name it. Crisscrossed the country a bunch of times. I must have made a thousand stops. Been just about everywhere. Maine, Florida, California, New York."

"I'm from New York," said Fenton. "New York City."

"Is that so?" said Sam. "Interesting place, New York. Big cities never did agree with me too much, though. I like a nice, friendly, small town. Saw quite a few of them in my travels. Made myself a little living by selling my carvings."

"Carvings?" said Fenton. "You mean wood carvings?"

"That's right," said Sam. He reached into the pocket of his old jacket. "Like this."

He pulled out a small figure and held it out in the palm of his hand for them to see. It was a tiny wooden squirrel holding an acorn in its hands. Every detail of the animal had been carved, the fur, the eyes, the little paws holding the acorn. It was amazing to think it was actually made out of wood. Then Fenton remembered something.

"Hey, this looks a lot like a bird I saw the other day at Mrs. Wadsworth's," he said.

"Why, yes," said Sam, "I did do a little bird for May."

"May?" said Maggie.

"Sure," said Sam. "May Wadsworth. She and I go way back, you know. In fact, she was the one who introduced me to Emily. And she's given me a few hot meals since I returned to Morgan. Makes delicious oatmeal cookies."

"Why did you decide to come back?" asked Willy.

"Well, I thought I might be getting a little old for the road," said Sam. "And all these years of traveling, I always felt a kind of a pull, like someday I'd have to come back to Morgan. Who knows? Maybe I'll even settle down here. Nice people, plenty of scrap wood over at the lumberyard for my carvings."

"So you're the one who was taking the wood!" said Fenton.

"Why, yes, I didn't think anyone was using it," said Sam. "Say, is that lumberyard still owned by the Cregg family?"

"It sure is," said Willy.

Sam shook his head. "I remember there used to be a nasty little Cregg boy who would hang around there. A real little brat. I'm pretty sure his name was Wendell."

"*Wendell?*" said Willy. "That's Buster's name!"

"But that was a long time ago," said Fenton. "It couldn't have been Buster. He wasn't even born yet."

"Actually, Buster's real name is Wendell Junior," said Maggie. "So that must have been his father." She laughed. "I guess it figures Buster's father was a nasty kid, too."

Willy turned to Sam. "Do you really think you might stay in Morgan now for good?"

"Maybe," said Sam. He paused. "If I'm not haunted by too many old memories, that is." He looked down at the ground. "Life on the road's been getting a little tough. I've had some bad luck lately. Got robbed on a train, had some trouble selling my carvings. But who knows? Maybe things are about change for me at last." He reached into the pocket of his jacket and pulled something out of it. "May Wadsworth gave me a little present today."

He held out his hand. In it was the piece of petrified wood that Willy had found at the dig site.

"Hey," said Willy, "that's—"

But he stopped. He looked over at Fenton and Maggie, and back at Sam.

"That's supposed to be good luck, you know," he finished quietly.

"So they say," said Sam, beaming down at the little rock. "So they say."

"You know, Sam," said Willy softly, "you can stay here in the shack as long as you like. It's fine with me."

"Why, thank you," said Sam, smiling a little. "I think I may take you up on that, at least for the night."

"Wow," said Maggie, looking at her watch. "I'd better get going. Hey, listen, Sam, there's plenty of food here in this bag if you get hungry."

"Why, thank you," said Sam. "I had my supper at May's, but I just might want a little snack later on."

"I guess we should go, too," said Willy, standing up. He looked at Fenton. "We can just tell our parents that we decided not to camp out here after all. You know, that it got too cold or something."

"Okay," said Fenton, although he couldn't help wondering

if it was really such a good idea for them to leave Sam out here by himself. After all, he thought, they didn't even know him. But Willy and Maggie didn't seem worried about it at all. And, Fenton reminded himself, it was only the shack. It wasn't like they had invited Sam home with them.

"You can use this sleeping bag if you want," Willy said to Sam. "I'll leave it here."

"That's very kind of you," said Sam. "Thank you for everything."

"No problem," said Willy.

"Yeah," said Maggie. "Have a good night."

"Bye, Sam," said Fenton.

As the three of them walked out of the shack and into the moonlight, they could hear the soft strains of harmonica music beginning to play.

12

"I don't know," said Fenton the next day as he, Maggie, and Willy rode their bicycles up Sleeping Bear Mountain road toward the dig site. "Do you guys really think it was a good idea to just leave Sam in the shack like that?"

"Sure," said Willy. "I think he was probably okay there. I mean, I know he's kind of old and stuff, but I bet he's used to sleeping in strange places. Besides, I did leave him my sleeping bag."

"Yeah," said Maggie. "And remember, he had all that food to eat. I'm sure he was fine."

"That's not really what I meant," said Fenton.

"Well, what did you mean, then?" asked Maggie, pedaling by him.

"Well," said Fenton, "it's just that we don't even really know him or anything. He's basically a stranger."

"He's not a stranger," said Willy. "He's from Morgan."

"That doesn't mean anything," Fenton pointed out. "And besides, even if it did, how do we know it's true?"

"What do you mean?" asked Willy. "Of course it's true. Remember? Sam built the shack."

"Fen, I think it's pretty clear we can trust him," said Maggie. "He said he's a friend of Mrs. Wadsworth's."

"Yeah," said Willy. "And if he wasn't a good friend, why would she have given him the petrified wood?"

"Okay, I guess you're right," said Fenton as they turned off Sleeping Bear Mountain Road and onto the dirt road that led to the dig site.

He supposed it made sense, what Maggie and Willy had said. The petrified wood was pretty good proof that Sam was a friend of Mrs. Wadsworth's. And it seemed pretty clear that Sam had been at the rock museum shortly before Fenton, Maggie, and Willy had gotten there that day. Fenton had heard the harmonica music himself.

In a way it was kind of like the story his mother had told him, about the people she had met in India and gone out to dinner with. What was it she had said? That New Yorkers were sometimes too distrustful of people they didn't know. Maybe Fenton just needed to be more of a Morganite.

"I guess you guys are right," said Fenton as they approached the dig site. "But if Sam is going to stay around a while, I do think it might be smart for us to tell our parents about him."

"Okay," said Willy. "That sounds like a good idea. We could even introduce him to them. After all, there may not be too many people left in Morgan who Sam knows. If he does decide to settle down here, he'll probably need some new friends."

"I don't know," said Maggie. "Somehow I can't really imagine my mother being friends with anyone like Sam. She probably wouldn't think too much of someone who had just been traveling around by himself for that long."

"I think going all over the place like that must be cool," said Fenton. "Maybe when I grow up, I'll travel around to dig sites all over the world."

"That would be fun," agreed Maggie. "You could write a book about it. You know, telling about all the different amazing dinosaur discoveries you'd seen."

"Yeah, I guess," said Fenton, pulling up next to the trailer.

He waved to his father, Charlie, and Professor Martin, who were standing by the nest-excavation site.

"I don't know what I'd say about *this* find, though," he said. "Eggs that were too small for the dinosaurs that were supposedly in them; it wouldn't make much sense."

"That's for sure," said Willy.

"Yeah," said Maggie as they laid their bikes on the ground. "About as much sense as one of those silly stories from *Ghostimonials.*"

"Hey, come on, you guys," said Willy as they headed toward the nest. "You have to admit, that was pretty spooky out at the shack last night. You know, with the ghost from the pond, and the footsteps and everything."

"Squelch, squelch, squelch," said Maggie, laughing. "I guess it *was* kind of creepy though, especially since we had just found Sam's footprint in the snow a little while before that."

"Hey, yeah," said Willy. "I thought you said ghosts couldn't have footprints, Fenton. That ghost in the comic book had squelchy footsteps, so maybe he had footprints, too."

But Fenton wasn't listening. Suddenly, something about what Maggie had said made him start to think. What was it that Sam's footprint in the snow had reminded him of? Then he remembered—the indentation at the edge of the nest, the one he had started to uncover that day but never finished. The more he thought about it, the more things began to come together in his head.

"Oh, my gosh!" he said. "*Sam's footprint!* That's it!"

"What's it?" said Willy.

"Yeah, Fen, what do you mean?" asked Willy.

"The mystery of the nest!" said Fenton, breaking into a little run. "I think I just figured out the answer!"

13

"Calm down, son," said Mr. Rumplemayer. "Now show me just where you think this footprint is."

Fenton looked over at the portion of the nest he had been working on the other day. The large tarp that the paleontologists had used to protect the site from yesterday's snow lay folded on top of the nest's ridge.

"It's right there," said Fenton, hurrying over. "Under the tarp."

He pushed the snow off that corner of the tarp, then lifted it and pointed to the still partly covered indentation in the sandstone rim of the nest.

"See?" he said excitedly. "We have to uncover the rest of it right away, Dad!" Mr. Rumplemayer peered at the indentation for a moment, and then looked up.

"Charlie," he said evenly. "Why don't you bring that digging equipment over here so we can have a look at this."

A little while later Fenton, his father, Charlie, Maggie, Willy, and Professor Martin stood looking down at the footprint on the rim of the nest. The mudstone had been cleared away, and a long, slender, three-toed imprint was clearly visible.

"Well," said Professor Martin, "would you look at that!"

Charlie chuckled. "I'll be a monkey's uncle."

"It looks like you were right, Fenton," said his father.

"What's happening?" asked Willy. "I don't get it. Is that footprint from the dinosaur, or not?"

"Oh, it's definitely from *a* dinosaur," said Fenton. "But there's no way it's from a ceratopsian."

"Oh, yeah," said Maggie, looking down at the imprint. "Ceratopsians had kind of short, stubby toes, right?"

"Right," said Fenton. "And one of them was shorter, kind of like a thumb."

"Not only that," said Mr. Rumplemayer, "but ceratopsians had four toes, and this print was clearly made by a three-toed dinosaur."

"Well then, which dinosaur was it?" asked Willy.

"Actually, we'll probably never know exactly which one," said Professor Martin, "but there are a couple of things we can be pretty sure of, thanks to Fenton. First of all, it was probably smaller than a ceratopsian. Or at least it laid smaller eggs than ceratopsians did."

"Oh!" said Maggie. "I think I see. So the small eggs that were put back together didn't belong to a ceratopsian after all. They belonged to another dinosaur. A three-toed one."

"That's right," said Fenton.

"Wait a minute," said Willy. "Then how did those ceratopsian embryos get in there?"

"Well," said Fenton, "the way I figure it, the nest was first built by a ceratopsian who laid her eggs there. But those eggs never got to hatch. Probably something happened to the mother ceratopsian while the eggs were still incubating."

"Gotcha," said Charlie. "And that's where our little three-toed friend came into the picture."

"Right," said Fenton. "The three-toed dinosaur must have found the abandoned nest after the ceratopsian embryos were already dead and decided to use it to lay her own eggs."

"Yes," said Fenton's father. "That makes sense. As she was getting the nest ready for her own eggs, she must have crushed what was left of the ceratopsian eggs."

"And left part of her own footprint on the rim," added Professor Martin.

"Exactly," said Fenton.

"Okay," said Maggie. "So let me see if I get this. The eggs that were put back together were from the smaller dinosaur, the three-toed one. But then what happened to the eggshells from the ceratopsian?"

"The way I see it, they must have been broken up into pretty small pieces by all that activity going on on top of them," said Fenton.

"Which is why all the pieces we found in the bottom of the nest were so tiny," said Charlie.

"And since we naturally began reconstructing the eggs with the big pieces we had, what we ended up with were reconstructions of only the eggs that were on top," said Professor Martin. "Very nicely reasoned, Fenton."

"Yeah, Fen," said Maggie. "That was pretty cool."

"How did you figure it all out?" asked Willy.

"Well," said Fenton, "I had seen the beginnings of the footprint a while ago, when I was out here digging. I had meant to finish uncovering it, because I thought it could turn out to be an important clue to the mystery of who built the nest. But then that same day the piece of the skull was found. And since that told us for sure that it was a ceratopsian, I kind of forgot about the imprint. In fact, I probably wouldn't have remembered it at all if it hadn't been for Sam and *his* footprint."

"Sam?" said Mr. Rumplemayer. "Who's Sam?"

"Oh yeah, Dad," said Fenton, glancing at Maggie and Willy. "That reminds me, I do have one other thing to tell you about."

14

"I really wish you had told me about this right away, son," said Mr. Rumplemayer later, as he followed Fenton, Willy, Maggie, and Owen through the woods toward the shack.

"I know, Dad," said Fenton. "But I figured it was okay, since he knew Mrs. Wadsworth and everything. Besides, the other day on the phone Mom was saying that she thought people from New York probably didn't trust other people as much as they should."

"Well, she certainly had a point, there," said his father. "And I'm sure this old gentleman of yours is quite harmless, but still . . ."

His voice trailed off as they reached the shack.

"Gee, I guess we should knock," said Willy. He rapped on the door of the shack.

But there was no answer.

"Maybe he hasn't come back for the night yet," said Fenton.

"Hey, look!" said Maggie, pointing below the window, where they had first seen Sam's bootprint in the snow.

There, scratched into the dirt, were the words THANKS & SO LONG!

"Wow," said Fenton. "I guess that means he's gone."

"Well then, no harm done, I suppose," said Mr. Rumplemayer.

"I guess I should check, just in case," said Willy.

He pushed open the door, and he, Fenton, and Maggie peered inside.

"Nope," said Maggie. "No sign of him."

"Well, I guess I'll head back to the house," said Mr. Rumplemayer. "Fenton, you coming?"

"I'll be there in a few minutes, Dad," answered Fenton. He turned to Willy and Maggie. "What do you think made Sam leave?"

"I don't know," said Willy, sounding a little sad. "I really thought he might settle in Morgan."

"Maybe it was like he said," said Maggie. "Maybe there were too many memories here, haunting him."

"Yeah," said Fenton. "I guess that makes sense."

He walked into the shack.

"Hey," he said, suddenly spotting three small objects sitting on one of the crates, "what are those?"

Willy walked over to the crate and peered at the objects. "I think they're for us."

"Let me see," said Maggie, coming over.

Fenton stepped forward to take a look too. There, sitting on the crate, were three tiny wood carvings. Looking at them, there was no doubt about who they were for.

The first carving was of a horse rearing up in the air, its mane flying behind it in the wind.

"Wow," said Maggie, picking it up. "This is beautiful."

The second carving was a ceratopsian pawing the ground with its front foot. Fenton picked it up. Every detail of the animal was visible—the horns on its head, the frill behind its neck, and even the four stout toes on its feet.

"How amazing," he said, turning it over to admire it.

The third carving, the one meant for Willy, was the most impressive of them all. It was an exact miniature replica of the shack, complete with windows and slanted roof. And its front door was wide open.

"This is great, you guys," said Willy, looking down at the carving. Then, suddenly, he looked up. "But how did he know?"

"How did who know what?" asked Maggie.

"Sam," said Willy. He pointed at Maggie's wood carving. "How did he know you liked horses?"

"Gee, I don't know," said Maggie. "That's a good question. I didn't say anything to him about it."

"Hey, yeah," said Fenton, looking at his own carving. "And I don't think I told him about the dig site, either."

"Oh, I know," said Maggie. "Mrs. Wadsworth probably told him."

"Maybe not, though," said Willy.

"What do you mean?" asked Fenton. "That's the only logical explanation."

Willy shook his head. "There is one other possible explanation," he said.

"Oh, yeah?" said Maggie. "What's that?"

"Just think about it," said Willy. "You know, old Sam just appearing out of nowhere and then disappearing again like that. And knowing all that stuff without being told. You have to admit, it *is* kind of spooky." He looked at them. "It might even make a good story for *Ghostimonials*."

"Oh, no!" groaned Maggie and Fenton together.

Fenton made his way out of the computer animation room and left the Galaxy Studios building. Outside, as he was passing the lot where the stars' trailers were parked, he saw Justin coming toward him. Justin was walking slowly, and his head was hanging. In fact, he was so lost in whatever he was thinking about that he almost bumped right into Fenton.

"Hey, Justin, watch out," said Fenton.

Justin looked up, a worried expression on his face.

"Fenton, you've got to help me," he said. "Everyone is convinced that I'm the one who damaged the model of the ankylosaurus."

"Well, you have been pulling a lot of pranks," Fenton pointed out.

"I know, I know," said Justin. "And that's why everyone suspects me. But I'm not responsible for this one, or for *any* of the stuff that's gone wrong with the dinosaurs for the movie, I promise."

Fenton looked at Justin. Something in his new friend's face convinced him that Justin was telling the truth, the trouble with the ankylosaurus wasn't just another one of Justin's practical jokes.

"You've got to believe me," said Justin miserably.

"I do believe you," Fenton told him.

There was no doubt about it, something strange was going on at Galaxy Studios. And it wasn't a jinx, either. No, someone was definitely up to no good on the set of *Night of the Carnotaurus*, someone who wanted to sabotage the movie. And Fenton was determined to figure out who it was and why they were doing it.

Look for **DINOSAUR DETECTIVE #6** and the rest of the series in your local bookstore, or call the toll-free number 1-800-877-5351.

Join Fenton Rumplemayer in more of his awesome adventures in the Dinosaur Detective series.

#1 On the Right Track

Fenton feels out of place when he first moves to Wyoming. But when a mysterious set of dinosaur tracks turns up, he's right at home. Hooked up by computer to his old pal Max in New York, and ably assisted by a new friend, Fenton tackles a case that has the local scientific team baffled.

#2 Fair Play

Fenton is the new kid in his class in Wyoming, and the bully has chosen him to pick on. But Fenton and his new friend Maggie have a great project for this year's Dinosaur Fair, and they're hot on the trail of a fossil that's missing from his father's dinosaur dig. Can Fenton and his friends find the missing piece, foil the bully, and still have their project ready in time for the fair?

#3 Bite Makes Right

Can a dinosaur be part bird-hipped and part lizard-hipped? That's sure what Mr. Rumplemayer's new fossil find looks like. Fenton is stumped. And on top of that he's been adopted by a stray mutt that's making trouble for all of his friends. Can Fenton find a good home for the dog and solve the mystery?

#4 Out of Place

Max, Fenton's computer-whiz pal, comes from New York for Halloween. But the visit isn't as much fun as the boys expected. Max doesn't get along with Fenton's new friends, and he thinks the story of the town's founding is a big joke. He doesn't even like working at the dig site, where the paleontologists have found a dinosaur that seems misplaced in time.

Try some other dinosaur books from *Scientific American Books for Young Readers*—

Jack Horner: Living With Dinosaurs
by Don Lessem, from the new Science Superstars series.

Jack Horner found his first fossil when he was eight years old. From that day on, he knew exactly what he wanted to do when he grew up—study dinosaurs. But his dream looked like it was over after he flunked out of college—seven times!

Author Don Lessem, founder of the Dinosaur Society and a friend of Jack Horner, tells the stranger-than-fiction story of a man who followed his own path to become one of the world's leading dinosaur experts, the real-life hero behind the scientist in the book and movie *Jurassic Park*.

Colossal Fossil
The Dinosaur Riddle Book by the Riddle King himself, Mike Thaler

- What dinosaur was a great boxer?

- What dinosaur played video games?

- What do you call a prehistoric Girl Scout?

Find the answers to these riddles and many more inside this wacky book about the most fascinating creatures to walk (shake?) the Earth.

If you like the Dinosaur Detective series . . .
Join Mathnet Casebook detectives George Frankly and Pat
Tuesday as they use their powers of reasoning to crack
confounding cases—and jokes, too.

#1 The Case of the Unnatural

Roy "Lefty" Cobbs is making a spectacular comeback for the
River Vale Rowdies. His batting and pitching averages have never
been better. In fact, they're too good to be true—which is why Lefty's
pal Babs Bengal suspects foul play. DUM DEE DUM DUM.

#2 Despair in Monterey Bay

Lady Esther Astor Astute is in despair—and no wonder. Her
priceless Despair Diamond has disappeared. The Mathnetters go
undercover—and underwater—to catch the thief. But their case
won't hold water until they turn to the tides. Something's fishy in
Monterey Bay. DUM DEE DUM DUM.

#3 The Case of the Willing Parrot

The late great movie star Fatty Tissue left his mansion to his
parrot. Now the wisecracking bird is doing some strange squawking.
Is it one of Tissue's infamous math games or a clue to a much bigger
mystery? Soon the Mathnetters are up to their Fibonacci numbers in
haunted corridors, birdnapping, and cryptic messages, as a clever
swindler tries to feather his own nest. DUM DEE DUM DUM.

#4 The Case of the Map With a Gap

Ten-year-old cowboy Bronco Guillermo Gomez is searching for
the long lost loot of the notorious Saddlesore Capone. He knows it
lies somewhere in the ghost town of Mulch Gulch. But he only has
half of the treasure map, and someone sinister is on his trail. Can the
Mathnetters help him fill in the gap? DUM DEE DUM DUM.

#5 The Case of the Mystery Weekend

George and Pat are going to play "Sherlock Condo" and "Dr. Whatzit" at a Mystery Weekend Party. But one wrong turn leads them to Wit's End, a sinister mansion presided over by the butler, Peeved. Strange things begin to happen as the guests disappear one by one. Who extracted Kitty Feline, world-renowned dentist? Who snipped short the song of jazzman Miles Reed? And how did soap star Sally Storm slip away? Can George and Pat out-math the mastermind behind it all? DUM DEE DUM DUM.

#6 The Case of the Smart Dummy

It's a case of mistaken cases! Ventriloquist Edgar Bergman is dumbfounded when he loses his luggage with Lolly, his dummy, inside. Instead, he's left holding the bag, and it's full of stolen money. The only one who's talking is Edgar's other dummy, Charlie McShtick, and he says Edgar is innocent. Is Edgar in the act or can Pat and George find out who's pulling the strings? DUM DEE DUM DUM.